Marky

Missy

Mr. Stevens

Mrs. Stevens

Sally Anne

Ol' Jack

First Edition. 10 9 8 7 6 5 4 3 2 1

First Printing 2000

Illustrations are water color style

Book design by Janet Long.

Body copy typeface is Kid Print Bold.
Title typefaces are Quaint and Tenace Regular

Publishers Cataloging-in-Publication Data
Prepared by Blessing Our World, Inc.

Library of Congress Card Number: 99-091779

Luke, Deanna, 1948–

Marky and The Rat / by Deanna Luke; illustrated by Lynne Chambers

Marky and The Rat is a series story of a boy and his adventures with his family and friends. The classroom rat teaches Marky about a change of heart.
For children, ages 7–11.

LCCN 99-091779 ISBN 1-928777-07-4

[1. Picture Books for Children 2. Prose and Children]
I. Chambers, Lynne, Ill.   II. Title

Printed in Hong Kong

Published 2000 by
SAN 299-8920
Blessing Our World, Inc.
P.O. Box 642
Palestine, Texas 75802-0642

Protecting the Minds
of Our Future

Visit our website at http://www.blessworld.com

Written by
Deanna Luke

Illustrated by
Lynne Chambers

Designed by
Janet Long

Blessing Our World, Inc.

P.O. Box 642 • Palestine, Texas 75802-0642

Hi! I'm Marky. Marky
Stevens that is. I have to
wear my coat every day because
so cold outside now. That means Christmas is com
but I don't have any money. That's a big problem

Petey is the white rat in Mr. Dantin's science class, and he has pink eyes...Petey, that is.

Mom has started playing Christmas carols in the house, and it always smells like cinnamon when I walk in. She hides what she bakes so I won't eat it up before Christmas.

All the girls squeal when Mr. Dantin brings Petey out of his cage for an experiment.

Missy is busy making presents for Christmas. Missy is my yucky sister. She's older than I am so she can baby-sit to earn her Christmas money. I don't know what I'm supposed to do for money.

Petey does neat things like ring a bell and wait for the piece of cheese that Mr. Dantin always gives him for a reward.

Dad is going away on a business trip for a few days. He usually tries to buy a present for us when he goes to a big city.

My friend, Sally Anne, sometimes has good ideas about making money. Maybe I'll ask her.

Petey is about six or seven inches long, but his skinny Ol' tail is about ten inches long, I think.

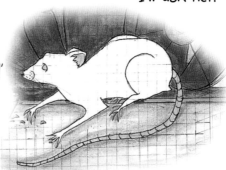

Sally Anne said her mom is paying her for extra work around the house. Yech!! I hate housework. Maybe Dad would pay me to rake the leaves.

During science today Petey bit Ol' Jack Martin on the thumb and Jack yelled, "Dang, dang, double dang," right in the classroom. He was so embarrassed in front of everyone because they all snickered at him.

Dad said he'd pay me one dollar a bag for raking leaves. Then he laughed like he just heard a joke. I never understand adults when they act like that.

Mr. Dantin told me to ask if my parents would let me keep Petey over the holidays, and he'll pay me a quarter a day. That will help me earn some Christmas money while I help Mr. Dantin at the same time.

Raking leaves is not too bad. It's even sort of fun, but I hate trying to put them in bags. No wonder Dad laughed. Maybe Sally Anne can help me.

Mom said Petey could stay as long as I keep the cage in my room, and Petey in the cage.

Sally Anne figured out how to hold the bag open with her heels and pull up with her hands while I rake in the leaves. We did fifteen bags today. Dad will really be surprised. I'm giving Sally Anne a quarter a bag!

Today was the last day of school so Petey came home with me in the car, and Missy squealed, just like the girls at school, all the way home.

Leaf raking is a great business. We did twenty more bags. Sally Anne loves helping me, too. Ol' Jack Martin says she just plain Ol' loves me. But that's not true. She's my friend.

If I take the cage close to Missy she cries.

Mom closed the guest room door yesterday and told Missy and me to keep out. Ol' Jack Martin dared me to go in, but I'm not. He'd like to get me in trouble right here at Christmas time. Sometimes I can't figure out if he's really my friend.

Petey is no trouble to take care of and feed.

Missy is always trying to see what I'm doing in my room. I wish she'd leave me alone and quit spying. I can't tell her though, 'cause I have to be good so I'll get piles of presents on Christmas.

Petey has a place to run in his cage, but it's a circle so he never gets anywhere.

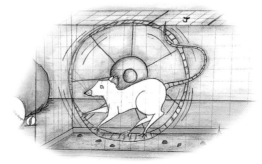

Dad owes me fifty-six dollars now for leaves. I owe Sally Anne fifty-six quarters. Dad's gonna be shocked. Now I'll laugh!!!

I saw Missy peeking at the door of the guest room this morning while Mom was gone to get a haircut.

Petey seems sad now, I guess he misses Mr. Dantin.

Missy was real surprised when I caught her. She came begging me not to tell on her. I made her cry and beg first, then we made a deal. She cleans my room, even under my bed, from now until Christmas.

Dad came in to take a look at Petey and let him play outside his cage, even though I told him Mom's rule about Petey staying in the cage.

Mom can't figure out why Missy's cleaning my room everyday now.

And, Sally Anne was so excited about the quarters she earned doing leaves with me. Ol' Jack Martin said he could have done the bags just as good as Sally Anne, if I would have asked him.

Petey liked being out and running and playing on the carpet instead of being in his cage.

Missy hates cleaning my room, because I leave dirty socks and stuff in the floor.

Dad was proud of me for figuring out a way to make my own Christmas money.

Mom is making fudge today. YUM!!! She let
me lick the pan.

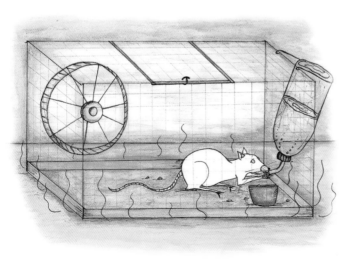

Petey's cage
smells sort of
bad, so I don't
think Missy is
changing the
sawdust and
paper each day
'cause she's
afraid of him.

Ol' Jack Martin came up with a funny
plan. We hid in my closet while
Missy cleaned my room.

Petey was with us and we were going to let him loose to
scare her when she came over by the closet.

She made my bed and picked up my bath towel. Then she came by the closet to pick up my pajamas.

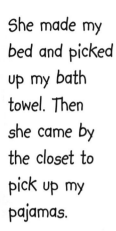

Ol' Jack Martin let Petey go right for Missy, and she jumped up on my bed, yelling and screaming her lungs out while Ol' Jack Martin and I laughed so hard our sides hurt.

Boy, was she mad. She yanked open the closet door and just stood there glaring at us with her hands on her hips. Her face was real red, too. I couldn't quit laughing though.

Petey was running all around the room, and he looked like he was having as much fun as Ol' Jack Martin and I were.

Missy said she was going to tell Mom, but I reminded her about me catching her peeking at her Christmas presents. She was mad and told me I wasn't fair. It just got funnier to Ol' Jack Martin and me.

Petey stopped running for a second and looked all around and then ran out the door.

Missy wouldn't m̲ₒ
to let us out of th
closet fast enough
Finally, I pushed p̲
her and ran to my
bedroom door to
in the hall. Ol' Jac
Martin and Missy
cam̲
to
too

Just as they got there, wouldn't you know,
Petey ran into the guest room and Missy
fell back on my bed laughing her head off.

"C'mon Missy, what do I do now?" I said. She just laughed and laughed. Then Ol' Jack Martin started laughing, too. I felt just like crying.

"Well, I just have to go in there and get Petey." (I hoped I sounded brave.)

ENTER!

I opened the door and tried not to look on the guest bed at all, because I knew I would be in a lot of trouble, twice.

Just as I spotted Petey and went in the room, Mom opened the back door and I knew I was a goner.

I was never so surprised as when I heard Missy take off down the hall for Mom. You could just tell she was trying to stall Mom for me so I could get out of the guest room.

Petey ran right to me, and I scooped him up and shut the door on the guest room tight.

"Go to your room for a minute, Missy." Mom's voice didn't sound a bit suspicious. Ol' Jack Martin and I just sat there looking at each other. Missy had come through after all.

Petey looked out from his cage like he knew he had seen freedom for the last time, and he was right.

When Mom had
unloaded all the gifts
into the guest room,
she stuck her head
in my room and
smiled. "It's safe to
come out now."

About that time Missy walked in my
room checking to make sure Petey
was in his cage.

I knew Missy had cleaned my room for the very last time from the look on her face. She was not the one over the barrel anymore. "I will not tell Mom anything that happened here today, but you will have to clean my room everyday between now and Christmas. Got that?" I nodded. (I probably would have agreed to anything just to keep her quiet.)

Petey was on his treadmill running and running.

Christmas morning finally came and we were all ready to open our gifts. I insisted Missy open my gift first.

Mom and Dad couldn't believe their ears. Everyone sat watching as Missy opened her gift. I had picked her out the prettiest earrings and necklace I could afford. She bought me a great pair of hugging monkey stuffed animals. Missy and I had gone together to buy Mom and Dad a set of gardening tools. It was our best Christmas ever.

I understood why Petey was so glad to be back in his cage, running on his own treadmill.

After all the gifts were opened and we were sitting around the breakfast table, Dad quietly said, "I think there must be a story someone would like to tell us about this Christmas." He looked from Missy to me and back to Missy.

Missy looked at me like I should keep my mouth shut about Petey's adventures.

"Well Dad, one day Ol' Jack Martin and I were going to play a joke on Missy." I looked at her and she shook her head no. So I just got very quiet.

Anyway, Petey has enjoyed his stay.

I guess Missy is a pretty good sister after all!

The End

About the Author

Deanna Luke has been writing since her youth. She is married to Jerry, and they have three daughters, Sunny, Keily, and Jennifer, and a son-in-law, Steve. They have four grandchildren, Nicole, Miles, Susannah, and Timothy. When her grandchildren were born Deanna began to look at several of her books for publishing. It is her desire for all children to have an opportunity to read books that offer excitement and pleasure as well as good morals and values. She graduated from Emmaus Road Ministry School in 1992. She has studied creative writing at the University of Texas in Tyler as well as private writers' conferences across the United States. She is dedicated to the Lord and the generational transfer of His love through her writing. She currently resides in Texas.

About the Illustrator

Lynne Chambers received her Bachelor of Arts Degree in Advertising with a minor in Art from San Jose State University in San Jose, California. Lynne has always included her art in various aspects of her life, creating free-form art, graphics and design, mural design, greeting cards and book illustration. Lynne desires at this time in her life to create for the Lord, applying her talent toward the generational transfer of the love of the Lord Jesus Christ.

About the Designer

Janet Long has a degree in advertising art and she spent the first ten years of her career in advertising. Her great love of books has led her to spend the last thirteen years as a freelance designer and illustrator of children's, educational and craft books.